D1113457

THE MYSTERY
AT
Mount
Rushmore

First Edition ©2010 Carole Marsh/Gallopade International/Peachtree City, GA
Current Edition ©November 2014
Ebook Edition ©2011
All rights reserved.
Manufactured in Peachtree City, GA

Carole Marsh Mysteries™ and its skull colophon are the property of Carole Marsh and Gallopade International.

Published by Gallopade International/Carole Marsh Books. Printed in the United States of America.

Editor: Janice Baker
Assistant Editor: Whitney Akin
Cover Design: Vicki DeJoy
Content Design: Randolyn Friedlander

Gallopade International is introducing SAT words that kids need to know in each new book that we publish. The SAT words are bold in the story. Look for this special logo beside each word in the glossary. Happy Learning!

Gallopade is proud to be a member and supporter of these educational organizations and associations:

American Booksellers Association
American Library Association
International Reading Association
National Association for Gifted Children
The National School Supply and Equipment Association
The National Council for the Social Studies
Museum Store Association
Association of Partners for Public Lands
Association of Booksellers for Children
Association for the Study of African American Life and History
National Alliance of Black School Educators

Once upon a time...

Hmm, kids keep asking me to write a mystery book. What shall I do?

Mimi

Write one about spiders!

Papa said …

Why don't you set the stories in real locations?

That's a great idea! And if I do that, I might as well choose real kids as characters in the stories! But which kids would I pick?

MiMi, PiCK ME, PiCK ME!

ME, TOO, MiMi, PiCK ME, TOO!

Christina

Grant

Pick me!

You two really are characters, that's all I've got to say!

Yes you are! And, of course I choose you! But what should I write about?

 National Parks!

 *SCARY PLACES!*

 **FAMOUS PLACES!**

FUN PLACES!

Disney World!

 New York City!

Dracula's Castle

 **GRAND CANYON**

On the *Mystery Girl* airplane ...

I can FLY Us anywhere!

Or aboard the *Mimi!*

Take me to the Forbidden City!

Or by surfboard, rickshaw, motorbike, camel ...

All great ideas! I can put a lot of history, MYSTERY, legend, lore, and laughs in the books! We can use other boys and girls in the books. It will be educational and fun!

Good stuff!

The Mystery Girl is all revved up—let's go!

You mean now?

LET'S GO!

And so, Mimi, Papa, Christina, and Grant took off aboard the *Mystery Girl* and America's National Mystery Book Series—where the adventure is real and so are the characters! —was born.

START YOUR ADVENTURE TODAY!

READ THE BOOK!

GO ONLINE!

TRACK YOUR ADVENTURES!

APPLY TO BE A CHARACTER!

Yikes! That was close!

Rats!

1
JACKALOPE JOKE

Christina sucked in a long breath of fresh air through her back seat window. Her straight brown hair whipped across her shoulders, strands twirling like a tornado. The cool wind whooshed in through all four windows of Mimi and Papa's rental car.

"Sure is a nice day for a drive!" Mimi said. Her wide-brimmed, red straw hat kept the wind from tousling her short blonde hair.

Christina nodded as she stared at the stunning landscape darting by her window.

Wide open prairie stretched for miles with black mountains towering in the distance. The golden prairie looked like an ocean of waves with wheat taller than Papa! A small sign on the side of the road flashed by. FREE ICE WATER, 2 MILES AHEAD.

"Yeah, it's a nice day for a *boring* drive, I guess," Grant said. His curly blonde hair was always in a mess, especially with the windows rolled down. Grant clenched his stomach with crossed arms. "But, after that long flight, I'm ready for LUNCH!"

"Sorry the *Mystery Girl* didn't have an in-flight meal!" a voice boomed from the driver's seat. Papa glanced in the rearview mirror and smirked at Grant from beneath his big, black Stetson cowboy hat.

Grant and Christina had spent the morning flying from Peachtree City, Georgia to the small town of Keystone, South Dakota with their grandparents, Mimi and Papa. Papa, the cowboy pilot, often chauffeured his wife and grandkids in his little red and white airplane, the *Mystery Girl*. Mimi was on yet another trip to research a new children's mystery book she was writing about Mount Rushmore.

They'd been traveling since before dawn, and hadn't stopped yet. When the *Mystery Girl* had touched ground, the four grabbed a rental car, checked into the local hotel, and hit Interstate 90 for a crash course in South Dakota tourism.

"So when are we going to see those four big noses?" Grant asked, still holding his growling stomach.

"You mean Mount Rushmore?" Mimi corrected.

"Yeah, the four big noses," Grant said. "Full of rock boogers, I bet!"

"Mount Rushmore is a lot more than four big noses," Christina explained. "It's a carving of four of America's greatest presidents."

"That's right," Mimi said, turning in her seat to face her grandkids. She adjusted the coat of her bright red suit. "Can you guys name the four presidents?"

"George Washington!" Grant said confidently. He folded his arms and eyed his big sister like a know-it-all.

"Right! What about the other three?" Mimi asked, patting the knee of Grant's wrinkly jeans.

"Ummmmmm," Grant stalled.

"Thomas Jefferson, Abraham Lincoln, and Theodore Roosevelt," Christina answered promptly. She smiled at her brother with the same know-it-all look.

"That's right!" Mimi said, always impressed by her grandchildren's intelligence.

"Now, can anyone tell me why the sculptor, Gutzon Borglum, picked those four presidents?" Mimi asked.

"Butzom Gorglum?" Grant muttered

"Aw, now, Carole, stop pop-quizzin' the young'uns," Papa interrupted in his smooth Southern drawl. He slowly pulled the car to a stop in front of a long wooden building with a front porch. The sign above said WALL DRUG STORE. "We're here!"

"What is *that*?" Grant asked, intrigued by a large statue in front of the store.

"That, Grant, is a jackalope, the fiercest of prairie predators!" Papa said. The statue resembled a larger-than-life brown rabbit with huge antlers. There was even a plastic saddle on its back. Grant's eyes widened in shock.

"Oh stop it, Papa," Mimi said, eyeing her mischievous husband. She put her hand on Grant's shoulder. "There's no such thing as a jackalope, Grant. It's just silly prairie folklore."

"I knew that!" Grant insisted. He shrugged Mimi's hand off his shoulder, ran toward the giant rabbit statue and shimmied up into the saddle. "Hey, Mimi," Grant called down. "Take my picture!"

Grant posed like a true cowboy with the reins of the jackalope in both hands.

"So, what is this place?" Christina asked Mimi as Papa helped Grant down.

"This is Wall Drug Store," Mimi answered. "It's been around the southern part of South Dakota since the Great Depression. Back then, they offered free ice water to travelers on Interstate 90 to try to get business. They put signs all along the road."

"I saw one back when we were driving!" Christina said excitedly.

"Well, the signs worked," Mimi explained. "Tons of people started visiting the drug store. It became a huge tourist attraction. Today it's not just a drug store, but a bookstore, museum, souvenir shop, Western-wear store, and restaurant."

"Did I hear restaurant?" Grant interrupted. He licked his lips.

"You sure did, cowboy," Papa answered. "And we're going to get ourselves a hot, juicy hamburger."

"And free ice water, of course!" Mimi added.

Mimi, Papa, Christina, and Grant made their way to the restaurant. Christina glanced at the long building of odds and ends and tourist attractions. Hundreds of people swarmed the place, sifting through tables of clothes and taking pictures with a small model of Mount Rushmore.

As Christina walked into the cool air-conditioned restaurant, she had an eerie feeling she was being watched. She quickly glanced behind her at the people walking past outside. When she did, her eyes met those of a short, stout, gray-haired woman, who seemed to be staring menacingly right at her!

2
NOT YO GREASY GRANDMA!

Christina couldn't help but stare back. The woman wore a uniform of forest green shorts, a matching button-up shirt, and a tan safari hat. Christina noticed it looked a lot like a park ranger's uniform, but she quickly dismissed the thought. She'd never seen a woman with gray hair and finely wrinkled skin working as a park ranger. This woman looked like she should be a grandmother baking cookies in her housecoat!

"Scarlett!" Mimi exclaimed. She smiled and hurried toward the woman. "I wondered what Christina was doing!" Mimi eyed Christina with a you-shouldn't-stare-at-others glare.

"You know this lady?" Christina asked. She couldn't hide the confusion in her voice.

"Sorry, sweetie," Scarlett said. Her face softened into a kind smile. "I hope I didn't startle you. I was just trying to see if that really was your grandmother here at Wall Drug."

"It's me, alright," Mimi answered. "We just got to South Dakota this morning and couldn't miss a stop at the famous drug store!"

"Yeah, did you see the jackalope as you walked in?" Grant chimed in. "It's the most dangerous predator on the prairie!"

"She knows there's no such thing as a jackalope, Grant," Mimi said. "Scarlett is a park ranger at the Mount Rushmore National Memorial."

Grant's bright blue eyes grew wide.

"*You're* a ranger?" Grant said.

Christina nudged Grant with her elbow and put her index finger to her lips for a *shhhh!*

"That's OK," Scarlett said. "I know I'm not a typical park ranger. In fact, I'm the oldest park ranger at Mount Rushmore. I've worked there for almost 45 years!"

"Wow! That's like forever!" Grant said.

"Well, not quite forever, but it is a long time," Scarlett admitted.

"So, why were you looking for Mimi?" Christina asked. She was beginning to like Scarlett. Not many women would be brave enough to have Scarlett's job at that age.

"Well, Carole—I mean your Mimi—called me about researching a new book she's writing," Scarlett said. "We're very excited to have a children's mystery book written about Mount Rushmore!"

"Scarlett has been very helpful in planning our trip," Mimi said. "She told us the best places to visit!"

"Like the Wall Drug Store restaurant?" Grant said. "Those burgers smell DE-licious. I hear them calling my stomach!" Grant let his nose follow the scent back to the restaurant door.

"We'd better go inside and get some grub before Grant faints from starvation," Papa joked. "Would you like to join us, Scarlett?"

Inside the cool, dark restaurant, Christina felt as if she had accidentally walked onto the set of an old Western movie. Shiny wood paneling stretched from floor to ceiling. Giant Native American statues were carved into huge tree logs that served as columns. A waitress, dressed in cowboy boots and a pink cowboy hat, led them to their table.

Everyone ordered juicy cheeseburgers and heaping baskets of French fries. They gobbled their scrumptious lunch in silence.

"So why in the world would someone carve a bunch of faces into a mountain?" Grant suddenly mumbled between bites.

"Not just anyone," Scarlett explained. "Gutzon Borglum was a famous sculptor who started the project in 1927. He worked on the carving his whole life until he died at the age of 73. His son Lincoln took over and finished the carving in 1941."

"So he never got to see Mount Rushmore like it is today?" Christina asked. She felt sad for Gutzon.

"Never," Scarlett said. "But Gutzon was confident his son could finish it. Now Gutzon's life dream is one of the most visited attractions in the United States!"

"Cool!" Grant said. "But I still don't understand. Why carve giant faces into a rock?"

"Gutzon wanted to honor the great leaders of the United States," Mimi said. She winked at Scarlett. "I've done a little research already."

"Mimi's right," Scarlett said. "Each president stands for a different American heritage. George Washington represents the birth of the nation because he was the first president. Thomas Jefferson represents the growth of the nation because he organized the Louisiana Purchase. Abraham Lincoln represents the preservation of the nation because he helped end the Civil War. And Theodore Roosevelt represents the United States' role in the modern world because he gained control of the Panama Canal."

Grant only half-heard Scarlett's detailed explanation. He was too distracted with slurping the dripping melted cheese from his burger.

SCREECH! Grant pushed his chair back from the table, rubbed his belly in satisfaction, and hopped to his feet.

"Well, I'm off to find souvenirs. Want to come, Christina?" Grant asked.

"Go ahead, you two," Mimi said.

Just outside, Christina found a rack of T-shirts and sorted through them.

"Whoa!" Grant yelled. "Look at that!" He raced to a table covered with tiny furry rabbits with antlers.

"Jackalopes!" Grant shouted. "I know what I'm getting!" He grabbed a chocolate-brown and white stuffed jackalope. "I betcha I can fool all my friends back home with this one!" Grant stuffed the jackalope under his arm and headed toward a shiny belt buckle display.

"What do you think about a big G right here?" Grant asked, pointing to the buckle of a black leather belt perched on his bony hips.

"I don't know if you're enough of a cowboy for that," Christina answered. She stared at the huge collection of crystal-encrusted belt buckles as big as her hand.

"This place is incredible!" Grant said. He was mesmerized by the rows and rows of candy, T-shirts, cowboy boots, baseball caps, key chains, and playing cards. The store seemed to stretch on forever.

"Yeah, it's nice to just be a tourist and not on some mystery mission!" Christina said.

"Yeah, no mysteries or villains, just the wide, open prairie, and the Wild, Wild West!" Grant said trying to sound like a rough, tough cowboy. "Hey, look at these!"

Grant pointed to a metal wall covered with magnets of all different shapes, colors, and sizes. Plastic outlines of South Dakota shouted, "You are Here!" Faces of four presidents stared at the kids from hundreds of miniature, gray replicas of Mount Rushmore.

"I could stare at this wall for hours and never see all these magnets!" Grant said. Christina nodded. As she scanned the wall, she spied a magnet that looked different from the others. It was bigger and looked more like a bathroom tile than a magnet. The surface was smooth, white porcelain.

"Look at that one!" Christina said, pointing to the strange souvenir.

"It's got something written on it," Grant said. "What does it say?"

Christina hadn't noticed the inscription. She stood on her tiptoes and strained her eyes to read the minuscule handwriting in faded black paint.

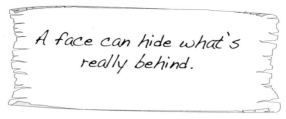

A face can hide what's really behind.

"Huh, well, a good word of wisdom, I guess," Grant said. He fingered a foam magnet of Abraham Lincoln's head.

"Grant, I don't think that smooth one is a magnet," Christina said. She suddenly sounded concerned.

"Well, it's sticking on the metal *magnet* wall. What else could it be?" Grant asked.

"I don't think it's *sticking* to the wall," Christina said. "I think it's *plastered* into the wall, like a tile. Plus, the writing looks really old."

"You're right. Who would buy such an ugly thing?" Grant said, still not catching on to his sister's logic.

"Grant," Christina said, annoyed. "I don't think it's for sale. I think someone put it there on purpose. I think it's a...a...clue!"

"Oh great," Grant said. "Here we go again. Why does there have to be a mystery everywhere we go?"

As the kids stared at the mysterious tile, Mimi, Papa, and Scarlett entered the souvenir shop.

"Let's head-em-up and move-em-out!" Papa boomed.

Christina absentmindedly followed Papa to the car. Was the tile really a clue or was it just her imagination? As she walked away, deep in thought, she didn't notice Scarlett behind her, glaring at the mysterious tile!

3
BAD LADS

"Buckle up!" Papa said as he eased the car back onto Interstate 90.

"Wait, what about Scarlett?" Christina asked. She didn't want to leave Mimi's new friend all alone at Wall Drug Store.

"Scarlett had to get back to work," Mimi said. "But don't worry, she told me the next best stop to visit—the Badlands!"

"What's the Badlands?" Christina asked.

"It's a place," Mimi explained. "A geological wonder, actually! And we're almost there," Mimi pointed to a sign on the highway. BADLANDS 10 MILES. "I think you'll understand once you see it."

The sun hung low in the sky and spread a dusty hue of light purple across the long, straight road ahead of them. Christina thought the golden **acreage** of the prairie would never end. But as Papa turned a corner of the highway, she saw something different in the distance. The prairie grass ended and a huge field of rolling rock hills and sharp rock spires emerged.

When Papa turned off Interstate 90, Christina noticed the road sign said BADLANDS LOOP. Ahead was a maze of rocks. She peered out her window at a huge rock hill striped with different colored layers. Purple, orange, and white seemed to glow from the rock.

"Look!" Grant said. He pointed toward a large stone archway on his side of the car. "I've never seen a rock like that before!"

"Why does the rock look like that, Mimi?" Christina asked.

"Historians believe this area used to be under water," Mimi said.

"You mean we're like 20,000 leagues under the sea *right* now?" Grant asked.

"Yes, I guess you could look at it that way." Mimi answered. "Except there hasn't been an ocean here for thousands of years."

In the distance, Christina spied a rock with a pointed tip jutting out of the landscape. It was as tall as a high-rise building. "That rock looks like a giant spear," she said.

"Many of the rocks in the Badlands have unique shapes because they're eroding," Mimi explained. "Years of corrosion made the rocks weak and crumbly. The rock washes away and creates some pretty interesting shapes—and colors. Different minerals in the rocks of the Badlands send off a colorful glow. Scarlett was right when she said the purples and oranges glow magnificently in the evening—"

Before Mimi could finish, everyone heard a loud *POP*! The rental car began to swerve out of control!

4
CAR TIRES, QUIZZES, AND COYOTES

Papa carefully guided the swerving car to a quick stop on the side of the road. Mimi and Christina sighed in relief.

"That was a close one!" Mimi said. "Good thing you're a careful driver, Papa!"

"What happened?" Christina asked.

"Well, darlin', it looks like we've got ourselves a blow out," Papa answered. Christina felt the right side of the car leaning toward the ground.

"Now that we're safe, I have to say that was pretty cool, wasn't it Grant?" Christina said. She glanced at her little brother. Grant was frozen in his seat clutching his seatbelt. A look of terror plastered his face. "Grant?"

"Uh, what, uh, yeah, cool, right," Grant said. He snapped out of his stupor and looked around. "Except now we're *stuck* in the *Badlands* at *night*! Not a good combination!"

"We're not stuck," Christina said. She eyed Papa with confidence. "Papa can fix it. Right, Papa?"

The four scrambled out of the car and surveyed the damage.

"Well, on a good day, yes, but unfortunately this rental car doesn't have a spare tire," Papa said. Christina felt her stomach sink. "Looks like we'll have to wait it out here until help comes along."

"Oh no!" Grant said. He hung his head in one swift, dramatic motion. "I was right. We're stuck out here all alone, with no shelter, water, or...food!"

"C'mon, Grant," Christina said. She patted her brother's back in encouragement. "Someone will come along soon."

Before Grant had a chance to complain about something else, a shiny blue minivan rolled around the curve ahead.

"Look!" Grant said. He waved frantically. "We're saved!"

The minivan pulled over and a tall man with two braids that stretched down to his waist stepped out. He wore a suede vest covered in tassels, faded blue jeans, and scuffed brown cowboy boots.

"Hi there. I'm Peter Running Calf Raines. What seems to be the problem?" the man asked.

Mimi stuck her hand out for a shake and smiled. "It's so nice of you to stop! Guess it's that good old South Dakota hospitality. I'm Carole Marsh, and it seems we've got a flat tire with no spare."

As the adults discussed tire repairs, the side door to the minivan slung open. Two kids about the ages of Grant and Christina jumped out.

"Look!" Christina whispered to Grant. She pointed at the kids walking toward them. In the lead was a tall girl with curly blonde hair. She wore blue jeans and a purple T-shirt with stars dancing across the front. The boy looked just like Peter Running Calf, the man who introduced himself to Papa. He had olive skin and long, dark hair in braids.

"Hey guys, got some trouble?" the boy asked. Grant and Christina smiled and nodded at the rental car sitting crooked on a cranked-up jack. "I'm Mato Standing Bear Raines," the boy continued. "I think you met my dad."

"And I'm Rory," the blonde girl said. She gave Christina a sweet smile.

"Hi!" Christina said. She shook Mato's and Rory's hands. "I'm Christina and this is my little brother, Grant."

"Are you guys from around here?" Rory asked.

"No, we're from Georgia," Grant said. "We're just here on vacation with our grandparents, Mimi and Papa." Grant pointed toward the car where Papa and Peter struggled to turn a giant wrench while Mimi "supervised."

"What about you guys? Have you been to the Badlands before?" Christina asked.

"Of course!" Rory said. "We've lived in western South Dakota our whole lives. We know just about every nook and cranny of this neck of the woods. Lots of tourists come through here, so we're always answering questions and giving directions."

"Did you know archaeologists have found fossils of rhinoceroses, camels, and turtles in the rocks of the Badlands?" Mato asked.

"Cool!" Christina said.

"Are, you guys, um, brother and sister?" Grant asked. Mato and Rory giggled.

"Of course not!" Mato said. "Rory doesn't look anything like me!"

Grant squeaked out a short, embarrassed laugh. "Right, I was just joking," he said quickly.

"Mato and I aren't brother and sister, but we're best friends," Rory explained. "We hang out together after school."

"Yeah," Mato chimed in. "I live on a Sioux reservation so I go to school there. Rory goes to a public school in town. In fact, my people, the Sioux Indians, were some of the first to call this area the Badlands," he continued. "They called it *mako sica*, which means 'bad land,' because it was hard to travel through."

"Where else are you going on your South Dakota adventure?" Rory asked politely.

"Well, Mimi's got the plan, but I think I heard talk of Custer State Park, and of course, Mount Rushmore," Christina said.

"Are you going to visit Crazy Horse?" Mato asked.

"A crazy horse?" Grant said. "Mimi didn't mention a crazy horse. Of course we're going to see that. What does it do? Walk backwards? Talk like Mr. Ed?"

"No. Not a *crazy* horse," Mato interrupted. "Crazy Horse. It's a monument a lot like Mount Rushmore. It's a work in progress, but when it's finished it will be a huge carving on the side of a mountain of Crazy Horse, one of the Sioux's most fearless warrior leaders."

"Wow! That sounds amazing," Christina said. "We *definitely* have to see that!"

"It's an important part of the Sioux's history," Rory explained. "Most people don't know all the awful things that happened to the Indians when South Dakota was first settled. This monument brings respect to the Sioux nation."

"Whoa!" Grant said suddenly. He sounded concerned.

"What, Grant?" Christina asked.

"It...got...dark!" Grant replied.

Christina, Mato, and Rory lifted their heads and looked around. Mimi and Papa's rental car was nowhere to be seen. They could barely see their hands in front of them. A thick, black blanket covered the Badlands.

"Oh my gosh!" Christina said. "How far did we walk?"

Suddenly, a long, high-pitched screech blared eerily from a distance. Then another. And another. Soon a chorus of growls, sneers, and howls sounded too close for comfort.

"What's that?" Christina said. She waved her arm in the dark, searching for Grant's hand.

"Those are coyotes," Mato said. "They're all over the Badlands."

"Will they hurt us?" Grant asked in his bravest voice.

"They never have before," Rory said. She tried to sound encouraging.

"Yeah, but we've never been lost in the pitch black in the middle of the Badlands before, either," Mato said.

Christina felt a chill rush all the way down her spine. Tiny goose bumps made her skin prickly.

"It's pretty cold out here, too," Christina said. She tried to stay calm.

"South Dakota is known for its chilly nights," Mato said. "Here, take my coat."

Mato wrapped his warm wind breaker around Christina's shoulders.

"Do you think Mimi and Papa realize we're gone?" Grant asked. His voice quivered.

"I know my dad will notice sooner or later," Mato said. His voice sounded optimistic. "We just have to wait it out."

HOOOOWWWWWLLLL! Another coyote howl made all four kids jump close together in a terrified huddle. Suddenly, a blazing light blinded them. Christina, Grant, Mato, and Rory didn't even have time to run!

42

5
NIGHT LIGHT

The light seemed to float through the air faster and faster until it surrounded the children with its glow. Christina shielded her eyes with her hand. Grant screamed. "*AAAAAHHHHHHH!* Get it away from me!"

When her eyes adjusted to the bright light, Christina realized it wasn't one light, but two. Suddenly, the lights clicked off and Mimi's voice echoed across the deserted Badlands.

"Christina, honey, are you OK?" Mimi rushed toward Christina and swooped her up in a big grandma hug. "Papa and I thought we'd lost you."

"Mimi!" Grant said. He jumped toward Mimi and almost knocked her over. "I thought I was a goner. How did you get here?"

"The light was from your grandparents' rental car," Mato explained. He surveyed the car and patted the passenger's side. "They fixed the flat tire."

Grant clung to Mimi like a barnacle to a whale.

"Well, I'd say that's enough excitement for one night," Papa said. He cranked up the car and motioned for the family to load up.

Christina hesitated. She didn't want to leave Mato and Rory. They were fun to be with and seemed to know everything about South Dakota. Suddenly, an idea hit her.

"Hey, Mimi," Christina said in her sweetest voice. "Meet Mato and Rory, our new friends."

"How do you do?" Mimi said.

"Rory and Mato aren't just nice people," Christina continued. "They're from southwest South Dakota. They've even been to the Badlands before. You know, it sure would be nice to keep them with us all the time, like our own personal tour guides. Plus, they'd be *excellent* for research." Christina grinned at Mimi.

"You don't fool me, missy," Mimi said, smiling. "But I don't see why we couldn't bring along a few friends. If that's okay with you, of course." Mimi looked at Mato's dad.

"I live right in Keystone, so you'll be close," Peter said. "I think I could spare them for the weekend. I'll drop them off at the hotel tomorrow morning."

The four kids slapped high fives. Christina and Rory hugged each other with a girly squeal.

"Well, it looks like tomorrow it'll be six of us in one tiny car," Papa said. "It'll be a tight fit in the front seat and the back seat!"

"I'm so glad you get to come with us!" Christina told Rory and Mato.

"And since we've been through a near-death experience and all, I guess that makes us like best friends!" Grant added.

"Yeah, and since I saw you scream like a little girl, I guess that means we know a lot about each other," Mato joked.

Grant lifted his scrawny arms and flexed his tiny biceps. "I just had a moment," he said. "I'm usually a manly man."

Mato and Rory giggled. But Christina was distracted by something on the side of the road shimmering in the car's headlights. It looked like a piece of glass. She stepped closer and found a smooth white tile cemented into the asphalt. Christina froze. Small black handwriting covered the tile, just like the one from Wall Drug Store. Christina slowly bent down to get a better look at the tile. She could barely make out the faded words in the glow of the headlights.

What lurks behind
me tells
the true story of the
country you see.

Christina had almost forgotten about the clue in Wall Drug Store, but now she couldn't deny that a mystery was unfolding. Two clues in one day couldn't be a coincidence. Since she couldn't **uproot** the tile from the asphalt, she yanked a piece of paper and a pen from her pocket and scribbled down the inscription. She slowly trudged back to the car, deep in thought.

"We'd better head back to the hotel," Mimi told the kids. "We've had a BAD night in the BADlands and I'm ready for some rest!"

After they said their goodbyes, Christina pulled Grant to the side. "Look at this!" she said. She shoved the paper into Grant's hand.

"What? Another wise proverb from my big sister?" Grant joked.

"No! I found another clue on the side of the road, on another tile, like the one in Wall Drug Store," Christina explained.

"Wow," Grant said. "Two clues in one day! You know what that means."

"Yeah," Christina said, sighing. "A mystery!"

Grant nodded and they jumped into the car. Christina whispered in Grant's ear. "Keep the mystery to yourself for now," she said. "I don't want Mato and Rory to worry."

As Papa drove down the long, dark highway, the car was silent. Grant was half asleep. But sleep was the farthest thing from Christina's mind. She looked out her window at the creepy black landscape darting by. Who could know they'd visit Wall Drug Store and the Badlands in the same day? Was someone following them? Christina couldn't help but think that her bad day in the Badlands might be an omen for the rest of her trip!

6
MOTORCYCLE MANIA

After a good night's rest, Mimi announced that they were headed to Custer State Park for research.

"We've been spending *a lot* of time in this car! My bottom's sore!" Grant said. It was his turn to sit in the middle and he was smashed between his friends like a sardine.

"That's one of the beautiful things about South Dakota," Mimi said, "its wide open spaces."

"There are some places in South Dakota where you can drive for miles and not see one house!" Rory said. "In the country, there are only a few people and they live miles apart." Grant thought of the line of houses in his neighborhood back in Georgia. He couldn't imagine not having a neighbor for miles.

"Yeah, South Dakota is flat with straight roads that seem to go on forever," Mato added. "There are some places where you can stand in a prairie of waist-high wheat, look all around you, and see nothing but more prairie!"

"That seems kind of lonely," Christina said. She pictured being stuck in a prairie that never ended.

"Or peaceful," Papa boomed. Papa loved the West.

"I'm sure anything's better than this," Mimi said. She pointed out her window toward the road leading to the small town of Keystone. Hundreds of parked motorcycles covered the sides of the road. They leaned on their shiny chrome kickstands at a perfect angle in straight rows like dominos. There was barely enough room for Papa's car to squeeze through.

"Where did they all come from?" Christina asked. She'd never seen so many motorcycles in one place! The sunlight glistened off hundreds of chrome handlebars. "I didn't see these when we pulled in last night."

"They must have arrived early this morning," Mato said. He didn't seem surprised by the swarm of bikes. "They're here for the Sturgis Motorcycle Rally."

"A motorcycle rally for surgeons?" Grant said, confused.

"No!" Rory said. She giggled. "*Sturgis*. It's the name of a small town just down the road from Keystone. Every year they have a huge motorcycle rally. People from across the United States drive their motorcycles here for a visit."

"We should get some motorcycles!" Grant said. He stretched his hands out on imaginary handlebars and growled,

"VROOOM, VROOOM. It'd be a lot more comfortable than this backseat!"

Papa eased the car down the small strip of open road between the motorcycles. He slowly rolled to a stop sign at the edge of town.

"At this rate, it'll take us all day to get to Custer State Park," Papa said. Mimi pointed toward a clearing in the road ahead. "I think it'll be better once we get out of town," she said.

While the car sat at the stop sign, Christina took a closer look at the motorcycles outside her window. Some sported short, thick wheels and sat low to the ground. Others were cloaked in chrome that sparkled like sequined gowns at a fashion show. Logos of famous motorcycle brands fought for attention on helmets, license plates, seats, and T-shirts.

Suddenly, a movement caught her eye. Christina turned to see a tall man with shoulders so big they looked like they were ready to burst out of his black T-shirt. He was wiping the side of his gleaming red motorcycle with a rag. The orange flames painted on the side glistened like fire in the hot sun. He wore a black leather vest, suede chaps, and a red bandana on his head. He flaunted a faded tattoo on his huge muscled arm that read, "I Love Harley." Christina wondered if Harley was the man's girlfriend. A scruffy patch of facial hair at the bottom of his chin spiraled down to his chest. His dark sunglasses hid his eyes, but Christina had an eerie feeling he was glaring at her.

Christina lowered her eyes and tried to ignore the man. She sighed in relief when Papa pulled away from the stop sign and began to pick up speed.

"Did you see that guy?" Christina said. She glanced at her friends in the backseat.

"Yeah, and what about the tattoo on his arm?" Rory said.

"Yeah, it said, 'I love Harley' in black handwriting," Mato said.

Christina began to wonder if the black handwriting on the tattoo could be the same as the writing on the clues! She couldn't help but think that man looked like a bad guy. But how could he know anything about her and Grant?

As Christina silently reviewed the clues in her mind she heard a loud *VVVVRRRROOOOMMMM* behind her. She turned to look out the back window. Following Papa's car was a loud motorcycle—with orange flames on the side!

7
TATTOO SNAFU!

Christina froze. Even with a helmet on, the man's red bandana crept down over his forehead. Christina whispered in Grant's ear as quietly as she could.

"Don't look now, but we've got company," Christina said. Grant impatiently turned in his seat and eyed the bright red motorcycle following close behind.

"Is that our creepy friend with the tattoo?" Grant asked.

"Do you think that guy could have something to do with you-know-what?" Christina said. She made a square with her fingers.

"No, what?" Grant said. He stared at Christina with a dumbfounded look.

"*You* know," Christina said. She tried to mouth the letters C-L-U-E to her brother without Rory and Mato noticing.

"Uh, guys," Mato butted in. "We're sitting right here. We can hear your conversation."

Christina let out a sigh and gave Grant a frustrated stare.

"Alright," Christina said. She couldn't keep the clues a secret from Mato and Rory any longer. "Grant and I have sort of stumbled on a mystery. We've been finding some strange clues on our vacation."

"Vacation?" Grant said. He looked at Christina like she was crazy. "This stopped being a vacation back at Wall Drug Store. So far, we've gotten involved in a mystery, broken down in the Badlands, and now we have a creepy motorcycle man on our tail!"

Christina nudged her little brother's side with her elbow to shut him up.

"So, you think the clues and the man following us could be related?" Rory asked. Christina could tell she was trying not to get scared.

"It's hard to tell," Christina said.

"Well, what did the clues say?" Mato asked.

"They both sound like old proverbs," Grant said. "Something about your face not telling what's behind and how behind something tells the story of our country. Or was it your behind doesn't tell the story of your face? I don't know."

"Right now they don't make a lot of sense," Christina explained. "Although one thing is a little **suspicious**. Do you remember that guy's tattoo?" Christina motioned to the man following them.

"Yeah, it had something written on it in black handwriting," Rory said.

"Well, the clues were written in black handwriting too, and I thought maybe the handwriting on the clues and the handwritten tattoo weren't a coincidence. Do you think this guy could be planting the clues?" Christina said.

"I don't know, Christina," Grant said. He scratched his head in deep thought. "You said you didn't see motorcycles last night. If they got in early this morning, how would he have time to plant the clues?"

"That's true," Christina said. She hated to admit it, but she was actually impressed by her brother's logic.

"I don't know," Rory said. "I say *he* did it." Rory turned in her seat and peeked out the back window, then whipped back around before the man had a chance to see her. "He's *really* creepy. Plus, why would he follow us like this?"

"True, but I just thought of something else," Christina said. "The tile clues we found in Wall Drug Store and in the Badlands looked like they'd been there for a while. They weren't just hidden. It seemed like they'd been plastered in place for years."

"Why would clues be that old?" Mato asked. "I thought clues were hidden on purpose, for people to find." Christina thought about clues she'd found in the past. Most were hidden so she and Grant would find them. These clues seemed like anyone could find them if they looked in the right places. Christina felt confused.

"Well, I know this," Grant chimed in. He pursed his lips and crossed his arms like an expert. "I've solved quite a few mysteries in my lifetime and one thing is always true—no two mysteries are the same."

Christina rolled her eyes at Grant, but she knew he was right. Every mystery she'd ever stumbled upon was unique. She'd figure this one out too!

VVVVVRRRRROOOOMMMM! Grant, Christina, Rory, and Mato jumped in unison in the back seat. The motorcycle behind them roared with acceleration. Suddenly it was side-by-side with Papa's car and a red bandana and dark sunglasses stared into the backseat window!

8
THE NAME'S DOG, PRAIRIE DOG

Christina was sure the man was going to reach over, open her door, and snatch her out of Papa's car. But as soon as she saw him, he was gone. The red motorcycle roared ahead of them, leaving Papa's car in a cloud of dust.

Christina relaxed in her seat and saw the sign for CUSTER STATE PARK flash by her window.

"We're here!" Mimi announced. "Kids, I've got a pretty exciting day planned for you!"

Papa pulled the car into a parking lot near a visitor center. Grant and Christina looked at each other with a grin. Mimi's "exciting days" were always the best. She usually tried to distract her grandkids with something fun while she researched her books.

"Since Rory and Mato live right around here, they know Custer State Park like the back of their hands," Mimi continued.

"That's right!" Rory said.

"So I asked them last night if they would show you the coolest spots in the park," Mimi said.

"And of course we agreed!" Mato said. "We couldn't pass up a day of fun with two new friends."

Grant and Christina smiled at Mato.

"So I'll leave you four to it!" Mimi said. She walked away with a skip in her step, tugging Papa behind her.

"Most people like to explore Custer in their cars because it's so big," Rory said. "But Mato and I have found that you see the coolest things hiking on foot along the park's trails."

"Plus, neither one of us has a driver's license," Mato joked. "The first place on our hike is the prairie dog town."

Grant stood up straight with interest.

"Did you say prairie...dog...town?" Grant asked.

"Yes," Mato said. He grinned at Grant.

"So there are, like, dogs that live out here in the prairie and make their own town?" Grant asked.

Mato laughed. "You'll just have to wait and see," he replied.

Mato, Rory, and Christina walked to a gravel trail that led into a lush forest. Rolling green hills next to the forest seemed to stretch on for miles.

"This place is beautiful," Christina said.

"Yeah, and there's lots more to see," Mato said. "Custer State Park is huge!"

Grant followed his friends down the trail, lost in thought. He pictured a town full of dogs living peacefully until the prairie bandits—two boxers and a bulldog—stormed in.

"Grant?" Christina almost yelled.

Grant snapped out of his trance and looked up. Christina, Mato, and Rory had stopped walking and were staring at him.

"Mato was trying to talk to you but you never answered," Christina said. She gave her brother a look that let him know he'd been accidentally rude.

"Oh, um, sorry. I didn't mean to be rude. I was just thinking about the prairie dog town," Grant said. "The boxers and bulldog were about to hold an innocent baby Chihuahua hostage when you rudely interrupted me."

"Huh?" Mato said. "What are you talking about, Grant?"

"A prairie dog town," Grant said. "You're the one who brought it up."

"Oh," Rory said. She realized what Grant was talking about. "You thought the prairie dogs were *actual* dogs."

"Yes," Grant said with confidence. "What else could a prairie *dog* be?"

"You're about to find out," Mato said. He led the way toward an opening in the forest. In front of them was a large field full of grass and small dirt potholes.

"Whoa," Grant said. "What happened here?"

"*This* is a prairie dog town," Rory said. She swept her hand across the landscape in front of them. It wasn't anything like Grant imagined. He looked closer at the pockmarked field. Every couple of minutes something that looked like a chubby squirrel popped its head out of a hole. Then Grant heard a high pitched barking noise screech across the field.

"What was *that*?" Grant said.

"That's them," Rory said.

"Prairie dogs aren't golden retrievers or Chihuahuas," Mato explained. "They're small animals native to the prairie. They're in the same family as squirrels except they're fatter, have smaller tails, and they bark."

"They bark?" Christina asked.

"It's their way of communicating," Rory said. "When settlers came to the West they named them prairie dogs because of their bark."

"Yep, some scientists believe the prairie dog has one of the most advanced forms of communication among animals," Mato said.

"Cool!" Grant said. He dashed and jumped between holes in the field. Every once in a while a prairie dog stuck his head out of a hole, eyed Grant, and shot back down in the ground. "I think this might be better than a town run by a golden retriever sheriff!"

"Prairie dogs are only a taste of the wildlife in Custer State Park," Mato said. "Wait till you see the buffalo and burros!"

"Buffalo? And burros?" Grant said. "You didn't tell me this place was so amazing!"

Grant hopped off to explore more of the prairie dog town and to **demonstrate** how to catch a prairie dog. Christina followed her little brother and peeked into different holes in the field. She thought it was neat how the prairie dogs dug their own holes to protect themselves. In some holes she could see the glowing eyes of a scared prairie dog hunched back in the corner.

"Grant's right, this really is amazing!" Christina said.

She kept exploring when something different caught her eye. One of the holes seemed shiny in the sunlight. Christina walked toward the hole and peered in. No prairie dog stared back. In fact, the hole looked like it'd been deserted for a while. Christina stuck her hand in the hole to feel around for something. Her fingers grazed across the rough dirt and then she felt it—something cool and smooth. Christina knew what it was without even looking.

"Grant, Mato, Rory!" Christina yelled. "I think I found another clue."

The three ran to where Christina was crouched.

"You...found...a...clue...in...a...prairie dog...town?" Grant asked, out of breath from his run.

"I think so," Christina said. She gathered some courage and leaned down to read the clue. Sure enough, a small white porcelain tile with black handwriting lay cemented into the dirt.

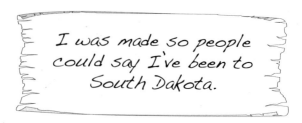

I was made so people could say I've been to South Dakota.

"It's another weird clue," Grant said.

"Yeah, that doesn't make any sense," Rory said.

Christina sat still staring at the clue. A sick feeling unsettled her stomach. Someone wanted them to find the clue, and the only people who knew exactly where they were going were Rory and Mato.

9
CAUTION!
BISON CROSSING

After an hour of exploring every nook and cranny of the prairie dog town, Christina, Grant, Mato, and Rory continued along the gravel trail. The forest cleared and the path swerved in and out of grassy rolling hills. The bright blue South Dakota sun beamed on the carpeted hills, glistening off each blade of grass. Christina tried to enjoy the breathtaking beauty, but she couldn't focus. She could only stare at Mato and Rory when they weren't looking. She couldn't stand it any longer. Christina tugged on Grant's shirt and motioned for him to stop walking. Mato and Rory continued ahead.

"I think Mato and Rory may be the bad guys!" Christina blurted out.

"What?" Grant said. "Mato and Rory? They're, like, the nicest people I've ever met."

"I know, but have you ever thought that maybe they're too nice?" Christina continued.

"How can someone be too nice?" Grant asked. "Why would Mato and Rory be bad?"

"Think about it, Grant," Christina explained. "We've found clues in strange places. Who would know that we'd be in those places to find them? Who was there in the Badlands? And the prairie dog town?" Christina's eyebrows arched in suspicion. Grant wasn't convinced.

"But they weren't with us at Wall Drug Store where we found the very first clue!" Grant said. "I just don't think Mato and Rory could be terrifying villains!"

"All I'm saying is keep your eye on them," Christina said. Grant shrugged his shoulders and scurried up to Mato and Rory on the trail. Christina lagged behind, still suspicious.

Suddenly, Mato and Rory froze. Rory turned and whispered for Grant and Christina to stay silent. Christina braced herself for Rory's confession to being the suspicious clue-planting villain. Then she saw it. Christina's mouth fell open in amazement. Standing in front of them was the biggest, hairiest animal she'd ever seen!

"That's a bison," Mato whispered. "As long as we're quiet and don't make any sudden movements, he shouldn't bother us."

The bison was taller than Papa with long, coarse brown hair. A rounded hump rose from its muscular shoulders and a scraggly tail whipped from side to side. Two curved horns jutted out behind its ears.

"His head is bigger than my whole body!" Christina whispered. She was terrified and amazed at the same time.

"Um...Um...Um..." Grant stuttered. He slowly lifted his hands and pointed down the sloping hill to the left of the trail. In the distance, huge brown bison dotted a flat prairie that stretched toward the horizon. They grazed peacefully on the soft grass.

"There must be hundreds of them!" Grant said. He forgot to whisper.

HUMMPPPHHHH! The huge bison huffed through his baseball-sized nostrils.

"Uh oh," Grant said. He stumbled backwards. "I think I made him angry."

The bison lifted his giant, hairy neck and stared at the kids. Grant shielded his eyes with his arm and braced himself for a charge. But the bison slowly lifted his hooves and trudged down the hill toward the herd.

"*That* was a close one!" Grant said. He watched the bison mosey toward a group that was busy chomping long blades of prairie grass.

"I've never been so close to an animal that big!" Christina said.

"I've lived in South Dakota my whole life and I've never gotten that close to a bison, either!" Rory said.

"I thought those giant, hairy, hump-backed cow things were called buffalo," Grant said, confused.

"Most people call them buffalo, but their real name is bison," Mato explained. "Bison are native to the Midwest. This herd is pretty small, actually."

"Small?" Grant said in disbelief. "There are at least 300 buffalo, uh, I mean, bison down there."

"You're right," Rory said. "But almost 200 years ago when settlers first arrived, *millions* of bison roamed the Great Plains. Now there are only a few thousand left. Custer State Park is home to a herd of about 1,300 bison."

"What happened to the rest of them?" Christina asked.

"When settlers began moving west they hunted bison for sport," Rory explained. "They killed them and left their huge carcasses on the prairie to rot. Settlers hunted so many bison that they almost became extinct."

"That's awful!" Christina said. "I'm glad enough survived so we could see them today."

"My tribe, the Sioux, hunted bison, too," Mato added. "Except we used every part of the bison for something—the meat for food, the fur for shelter and clothing, and the bones for tools. Once the white settlers began killing all the bison, my people had to find another way of life. We learned to be farmers instead of hunters."

"Did you eat the brains too?" Grant asked.

"*Ewww!*" Rory crinkled her nose and stuck out her tongue. "You haven't eaten bison brains have you, Mato?"

"No!" Mato said. "Of course I've never eaten bison brains. But I bet my great-great-grandfather did!"

"Cool!" Grant said. Rory and Christina cringed.

"We better get back to the visitor center," Mato said. "We don't want to get stuck outside in another dark, cold South Dakota night!"

The four turned on another path through waving prairie grass reaching up to Grant's shoulders. The setting sun cast a golden glow on the swaying sea of grass. For the first time, Christina really understood the verse about "amber waves of grain" from the song "America the Beautiful."

All of a sudden, the grass on the edge of the trail next to Christina began to rustle. Christina froze. The rustle grew louder and closer. The grass buckled beneath the weight of something lurking in the twilight. Christina knew whatever it was, something *big* was headed straight for *her*!

10

FRIEND OR BURRO FOE?

Christina tripped and stumbled to her knees. The rustling grew to a loud thunder. Mato, Rory, and Grant were too far ahead to hear the noise. Christina cowered in fear. She was stuck on the ground about be trampled by a vicious prairie animal. She tried to scream for her little brother, but her voice cracked. Just as a hoof stomped onto the path beside her, Christina saw Mato turn around. His eyes met hers.

Mato raced toward Christina, grabbed her arm, and yanked her off the path just in time to avoid a burro stampede.

Christina and Mato watched as a herd of burros dashed across the trail in a frenzy. Christina noticed they looked like horses but were shorter and smaller. Their gray hair was as coarse as the steel wool pads Mimi used to scrub her dishes, and their manes were short and spiky. Their hooves pounded the trail, kicking up a cloud of dust. When the last one scurried by, Christina sighed in relief. She hadn't realized she was holding her breath.

"Are you OK?" Grant said. He dashed to his sister's side.

"Yeah," Christina said, "just a little shaken up."

"I told you they were nice," Grant whispered to Christina. "Now do you believe me?" Christina knew her brother was right. How could Mato be bad when he had saved her life? She smiled at Mato.

"Believe it or not, those were the famous friendly burros," Rory said.

"Friendly? What a **subterfuge!**" Grant said.

"Subterfuge? Where in the world did you hear that word?" Christina said.

"My word-a-day calendar. I think it means deception," Grant said. "No, wait, maybe it was a spy. Or maybe a fugitive?"

"Well, it must mean a deception because they didn't seem too friendly to me!" Christina said.

"Naw, they were just in a hurry to get somewhere," Mato explained.

"Must be burro dinner time!" Grant said.

"I've seen the burros come right up to cars and let people pet them!" Rory said. "They're very comfortable around humans. I'm sure they didn't mean to scare us."

"Well, I forgive them," Christina joked. "Grant would probably run me over too if he was trying to make it to the dinner table."

"All this talk about dinner is making me hungry!" Grant said. His stomach gurgled and growled loud enough for the others to hear.

"My goodness, Grant!" Rory exclaimed. "Good thing we're almost back!" She pointed toward a small stone building in the distance.

As the four neared the building, they passed a green sign for the Peter Norbeck Visitor Center. The stone building resembled a fairytale cottage at the edge of a forest.

Mato opened the heavy wooden door of the cottage and let his friends pass through into a dark, air-conditioned room. A stuffed bison glowed in a harsh spotlight next to glass cases displaying maps and information about Custer State Park.

"Hello, darlings!" Mimi said. The sequins on her bright red jacket shimmered even in the dim light. "Back so soon?"

"We've been gone the whole day, Mimi," Grant said.

"My how the time passes when you're having fun," Mimi said. She scribbled one last thing in her notebook and slammed it shut. "I guess that's enough research for today." Christina thought she saw Papa smile in relief.

"So what have you four been up to?" a voice asked. Christina was sure she'd heard that voice somewhere before. She peered behind Mimi and found Scarlett standing near a lit display case.

"Miss Scarlett?" Christina said. "I thought you were a ranger at Mount Rushmore."

"Well, I am," Scarlett said, "but I wanted to help Mimi with her research today. When I got here, she told me you kids were off on an adventure. What did you find?"

Christina noticed Scarlett sounded a little too curious. She thought briefly about the clue in the prairie dog town but decided to keep it to herself. Before Christina could recap the day, Grant butted in.

"We saw prairie dogs! And as it turns out, they aren't dogs at all," Grant explained.

As Grant recited every detail of the day's adventure, Christina wandered around the exhibit inside the visitor center. The room buzzed with tourists eager to rest in the air-conditioning. Christina wondered if one of these unsuspicious-looking tourists could have planted the clue in the prairie dog town. Most of them looked innocent enough...except for a lurking shadow at the edge of the room. All Christina could see were two battered leather construction boots.

Christina stared for a second, trying to see the face that belonged to the boots. Suddenly, one boot stomped forward. Startled, Christina stumbled back. She felt something sharp press against her back. The boots and their owner slowly emerged from the shadow. Christina tried to retreat further but the sharp pain in her back paralyzed her. The boots stomped closer and closer. Christina was trapped!

11
A BISON, BOOTS, AND BFFS

Christina began to panic until she heard a familiar voice.

"That bison horn must hurt!" Scarlett said. Christina was relieved to see the daunting shadow was only Scarlett. She noticed that her construction boots were caked with brown dirt.

"Bison horn?" Christina said. She turned to see a stuffed bison's horn wedged into her lower back. In her fear, Christina had backed right into one of the exhibits!

"Try to be more careful from now on," Scarlett warned. She eyed Christina with a serious look. "No one's allowed to touch the exhibits!"

Christina was surprised by the harsh tone in Scarlett's voice. As she watched the elderly ranger walk away, Christina felt like a little kid caught stealing cookies!

"Everything OK?" Rory interrupted. She scooted close to Christina and squinted at the bison display.

"Sure, I was just studying the exhibits," Christina said. "I'm so fascinated by bison!"

Rory suddenly tensed.

"What is it?" Christina asked.

Rory slowly walked toward a display case of historical documents next to the stuffed bison. Her face looked pale under the spotlight.

"I think I found another clue," she said.

Christina felt a shudder roll down her spine.

12
RORY WORRY WART

Rory pointed to a shiny square in the bottom corner of the glass display case. It was almost hidden in the spotlight's harsh shadows. Christina crouched on her knees and squinted to read the inscription.

I may be hard as stone, but there's a passage to the center of my heart.

Christina whirled around and grabbed Rory's shoulders. "We have to get away from here," she said.

"Why?" Rory said. Christina's concern made Rory worry.

"Someone is planting these clues," Christina said. "Someone who knows where we've been, and maybe, where we're going. Chances are, they're in this room right now!"

"Really?" Rory looked around suspiciously. Families and groups of friends laughed and talked as they studied the displays. "All these people look like innocent tourists."

Grant and Mato shoved themselves between Christina and Rory.

"I found another clue," Rory announced.

"Whoa, two clues in one day again," Grant said. "This mystery is beginning to seem seriously mysterious!"

"So what did it say?" Mato asked.

"I don't think what it said is as important as *who* is saying it," Christina said.

"Christina thinks it might be someone right here in this room," Rory whispered.

"Did you tell Rory you thought it might be her and Mato?" Grant blurted.

"*Grrrannnttt!*" Christina groaned.

"Oh, I guess you didn't," Grant said. He laughed awkwardly.

"You thought we were planting the clues?" Mato said. Christina was surprised when his voice didn't sound angry. Rory giggled quietly. Soon all four broke out into laughter.

"Now that I think about it, I was silly," Christina said. "I've just been in so many mysteries I treat everyone as a suspect."

"So when did you figure out it wasn't us?" Rory asked.

"When Mato saved me from the burro stampede," Christina said. "I figured anyone who would save my life had to be a friend, not a foe."

"And friends don't plant creepy clues," Grant said.

"But someone did," Christina said. She focused again on the mystery at hand.

"Maybe we can figure out *who* if we figure out *what*," Mato said.

"What do you mean?" Rory asked.

"He means, we should figure out what the clues are about," Christina said. She smiled at Mato. "It's good to have some extra detectives on hand."

"Let's load it up!" Papa's voice boomed across the visitors center.

"I think that's our cue," Grant said.
The kids raced to the car. Grant claimed a back window seat and squished Christina in the middle. As she slid into the car, Christina saw the edge of a book sticking out of the pocket behind Mimi's seat. It was a history book about Mount Rushmore that Mimi must have picked up from Wall Drug Store. The picture of the four stone faces on the front of the book looked knowingly at Christina, as if they had a secret to tell her.

13
CLUE RUSH!

Suddenly, the clues began to fit like puzzle pieces in Christina's mind. She pulled a piece of paper from her pocket and wrote all the clues in order. "Faces" from the first clue, and "stone" from the clue she just found stuck out like sore thumbs.

"Oh my gosh!" Christina whispered. The car was quiet as it cruised down the smooth, flat roads of the prairie.

"What?" Grant said. "Did you see another burro?" Grant jumped in his seat and threw his arm in front of Christina's chest to protect her from a wild stampede.

"No, Grant!" Christina said. "It's the clues! I think they have something to do with Mount Rushmore!"

Christina showed Grant, Rory, and Mato her list of clues. "Read each one and think of Mount Rushmore," Christina said.

"'A face can hide what's really behind,'" Grant read carefully. "Face! There are four faces on Mount Rushmore!"

"Exactly!" Christina said. "Read this one, Rory." Christina pointed to the clue she found in the prairie dog town.

"'I was made so people could say they've been to South Dakota,'" Rory read. "Mount Rushmore was built to bring in tourists!" Rory looked up, excited.

"Exactly!" Christina said again. "OK, Mato, you read the last one, the one we just found."

"'I may be hard as stone, but there's a passage that leads to the center of my heart,'"

Mato read. "Stone. It seems so obvious now. Mount Rushmore was carved in stone."

"That's right!" Christina said. She couldn't hide her excitement.

"But I thought you found four clues," Rory said.

"We did," Christina said. "That's the only thing. I still can't figure out the second clue. It said, 'what lurks behind me tells the true story of the country you see.'"

"There's nothing behind Mount Rushmore, is there?" Grant asked.

"Nothing but more rock," Rory said. "No one's allowed to go behind the mountain except park rangers and maintenance workers."

"But we can't deny that the other clues have something to do with Mount Rushmore," Mato said. "They have to!"

"What are you kids discussing so intently?" Mimi asked from the front seat.

"Oh, just talking about how exciting Mount Rushmore is going to be," Grant said. He was being truthful, mostly.

"That's why I've saved Mount Rushmore for the grand finale of our trip!" Mimi said. She turned and joined the backseat conversation. "Tomorrow we will see something that may be just as amazing when it's finished, though."

"Crazy Horse?" Mato shouted.

"Crazy Horse!" Mimi said. "I can't wait for Grant and Christina to see that big old carving—in progress!"

The tone in the car changed from eerie to exciting. Everyone forgot about the clues and planned for the exciting day ahead. Everyone but Christina. She couldn't get her mind off the clues and the vanishing villain who was planting them!

14
DY-NO-MITE!

"I can't even begin to describe it," Mato told Christina and Grant on their way to the Crazy Horse Memorial. "It's not finished, but when it is, it'll be the greatest Native American monument in the world!"

"The best way to describe the Crazy Horse Memorial is to see it," Mimi said. She pointed toward a log building labeled VISITOR CENTER.

"We're here!" Mato said. As soon as Papa parked, Mato threw open his door and flew out. "I've been through this visitor center a million times, but I can't wait to show it to you guys!"

The four walked through glass doors into a lobby with a large information desk. Shiny knotted wood paneling covered the walls, floors, and ceiling of the room. Native American headdresses, clothing, and tools dotted the walls. A canvas painting over the information desk proudly displayed a man in a green button-up shirt and khaki trousers next to an Indian wearing a white feathered headdress.

"It's called 'The Promise,'" Mato said. He pointed to the large painting. "It depicts the reason why Crazy Horse was built."

"Because someone promised to carve a giant head into a rock?" Grant said.

"Not exactly," Mato said. "One of the great Sioux leaders, Henry Standing Bear, told the sculptor Korczak Ziolkowski about Crazy Horse..."

"Carjack Zoo Cow Ski?" Grant interrupted.

"Close," Mato said. He laughed at Grant's effort. "Anyway, Standing Bear said he wanted the 'white man to know that the red man has great heroes also.'"

"So they planned Crazy Horse to honor Native American leaders just like Mount Rushmore honors United States leaders," Rory explained.

"Why did they pick Crazy Horse?" Christina asked.

"Ziolkowski chose to carve Crazy Horse for many of the same reasons Gutzon Borglum chose to carve the four presidents on Mount Rushmore," Mato said. "Crazy Horse was a patriotic leader who fought for his people. He cared for the sick, elderly, and hurt. He died tragically at a young age defending Native Americans. It's an honor to the Sioux and a tribute to all Native Americans." Mato gazed at the picture and beamed with pride.

"Is that what I think it is?" Grant said. He pointed down the hallway at a large triangle.

"I think you're going to like that," Mato said, smiling. The four scampered past the information desk and hurried down the hallway.

"It's a real, live tepee!" Grant shouted. He lifted his eyes to the tip top where a vaulted ceiling framed the 12-foot-tall triangle. "This tepee could have a second floor!"

Grant and Christina gingerly stepped through the tepee's arched opening. Wooden poles as long and round as tree trunks propped against each other in a circle covered with thick canvas. Light glowed through a small opening at the top of the tepee.

"The hole at the top is to let smoke escape," Mato explained. He walked to the center of the tepee and sat on the floor Indian-style. "They usually made a fire for cooking and heat right about here. And they often made the canvas coverings of tepees from dried bison skin."

"It's like an oversized luxury tent," Grant said. "Would I love to have this in my room! Or in my backyard! Or in my garage!"

"It's sort of like a tent," Mato said. "But if you think this is cool, just wait!"

The four ducked out of the tepee and headed for another set of glass doors that led outside. Just outside the doors, the bright South Dakota sun glared off the blinding white stone of an enormous statue. The statue was a side view of an Indian mounted on a galloping horse. The Indian stared sternly ahead, his hair blasted behind him by the wind. He held his arm high and pointed past his horse. His muscular mount tossed its head in excitement, looking like he yearned to run even faster.

"It's AMAZING!" Grant said. He ran to the carving and rubbed his hand along the smooth white stone. Grant was tall enough to touch the hoof of the galloping horse. "I mean, you said the Crazy Horse Memorial was cool, but this is better than I ever imagined!"

"Um, Grant," Mato said. "That's not it." Mato pointed far into the distance to a rock mountain shaped in three stepping-stone tiers. "That's it."

Grant released the horse's hoof and peered at the mountain. "*Ohhhhhhhh,*" was all he could say.

Miles away, in the huge stone mountain, the silhouette of a giant face stared into the horizon.

"What you *thought* was Crazy Horse is actually a small-scale replica of what the final product will look like," Mato explained.

"I see it," Christina said. She stood back to look at the smaller replica with the mountain in the distance. The carved face in the mountain looked as tall as the high-rise buildings she saw in Atlanta back home. "It really will be amazing when it's finished."

"Why will he be pointing?" Grant asked.

"The sculptor designed Crazy Horse to point into the distance because of an old legend," Rory explained. "When asked where his lands were, Crazy Horse said, 'My lands are where my dead lie buried.' He's pointing toward his land."

"Wow, that's sad!" Grant said. "Do you think that's why his face looks so serious?"

"I like to think he's thinking of a brighter future for Native Americans," Mato said. "When Crazy Horse was alive, my people were kicked off their own land and forced to find new ways to live. They were often treated like savages; like they were less than human."

"But now Native Americans have a huge monument to honor their bravest leader!" Christina said. She was beginning to understand why Crazy Horse was so important to Mato.

"Only the face is finished so far," Rory said. "They're working on carving the horse's body. I always think it looks like someone paused a scene in a movie and carved it into a rock. It's so lifelike!"

"Yeah!" Grant said. "I wouldn't be surprised if the horse broke out of the rock any minute now and galloped away with Crazy Horse on his back!"

"That would go down in South Dakota history!" Mato joked. "A giant stone Indian riding a horse whose head is the size of a 22-story high-rise building!"

"Speaking of things that are giant," Christina said, "How in the world do they carve a *whole* mountain?"

"They use dynamite to blow away big chunks of rock, and chisels and hammers to carve details," Rory explained. "Sometimes I can hear the blasts all the way at my house!"

BOOM! BOOM! BOOM! BOOM!

A pounding sound jolted Christina from her thoughts. The beat throbbed in her chest. Christina couldn't figure out where the sound was coming from and began to panic. Then she remembered—DYNAMITE!

15
CRAZY HORSE BOOGIE!

Christina scrambled toward Grant and cowered behind his skinny body. "Grant, get down!" she said in a panic. "There's going to be a blast!"

Grant slowly turned and eyed his sister hunkered on the ground. "Christina?" he said. "*What* are you talking about?"

Just as Christina was about to blurt "DYNAMITE!" she saw the real source of the booming sounds. Four men in traditional Native American headdresses and leather loincloths circled behind her in a stomp dance. Two of the dancers beat huge bass drums strapped to their chests as the group slowly stomped to the middle of the visitor center deck to entertain the tourists.

"Um, nothing. I was just kidding," Christina said, embarrassed. She stood and ran her fingers through her tousled hair.

The circle of dancers stomped to a fast, pounding beat. The dancers without drums bent toward the ground, then raised their hands in the air in rhythm. Every few seconds one let out a low, soulful chant.

"I'm so glad you get to see this!" Mato shouted. "The dancers only come out at certain times to entertain guests. We came at the perfect time!"

"What are they chanting?" Christina asked.

"It's the traditional Sioux language," Mato explained. "They're chanting events from our history, like the legend of Crazy Horse. We have traditional dances like this at the reservation all the time. One of the most popular traditional dances is the rain dance."

"I love dancing in the rain!" Grant admitted. "But my mom doesn't like it so much when my shoes get wet and muddy."

"It's not a dance *in* the rain," Rory said. "It's a dance to *bring* rain in a dry season. I saw the elders in Mato's tribe perform it once when I visited. It was incredible!"

The Native American dancers drifted to the opposite end of the deck to entertain another group of tourists. Their rhythmic chants grew faint in the distance.

"I have an announcement to make," Grant said suddenly. He stared straight at Christina. "But you have to promise not to get upset."

Christina felt her stomach sink. What was her brother up to now? "I'll try," she said in her most sincere voice.

"I found another clue," Grant said.

"Where?" Christina asked. She kicked into detective mode and searched the ground around them.

"Remember when I thought the life-size statue was the real Crazy Horse?" Grant said. "Well, before I let go of the horse's hoof I felt something smooth. I'm almost positive it was another tile clue."

Before Grant could finish his sentence, Christina sprinted toward the statue of Crazy Horse. She smoothed her hand over the horse's leg and felt a cool square beneath her fingers.

"Got it!" Christina shouted.

"What does it say?" Rory asked.

Christina stretched around the back side of the horse's leg to read the inscription.

> I was the dream he didn't live to see; now people never visit me.

"Do you think this clue has something to do with Mount Rushmore like the others?" Rory asked.

"Grant!" Christina said. An idea clicked in her head. "Remember back at the Wall Drug Store restaurant when Scarlett told us that Gutzon Borglum, the carver of Mount Rushmore, died before it was finished?"

"Yeah," Grant said. "But if that's what the clue's talking about, the second part doesn't make sense."

"Grant's right," Mato chimed in. "Thousands of people visit Mount Rushmore every year. The clue says 'people never visit me.'"

"Did you see those dancers?" Mimi interrupted. Her red sunglasses sparkled in the South Dakota sun. "They were amazing! I almost broke into a boogie!" Mimi shimmied her arms in a little dance.

"Aww, Mimi!" Grant whined. "Not the granny dance!"

Mimi laughed and stopped dancing. "Are my four explorers ready to visit the grand finale of our trip?" she asked.

"We're going to Mount Rushmore today?" Christina said. She forgot about the clue and turned her attention to the event she'd been looking forward to since the *Mystery Girl* touched ground. "I can't wait!"

The four kids savored one last glance at Crazy Horse before they piled into the car.

"Mount Rushmore, here we come!" Grant hollered out his window as Papa drove away.

As they zoomed toward Mount Rushmore, none of the kids noticed the bright red motorcycle following close behind!

16
FOUR GIANT
STONE HEADS!

Papa pulled the car to a staircase that led to the entrance of Mount Rushmore. The kids scrambled out of the car while Mimi and Papa searched for a parking spot.

"We're here!" Rory announced. "Mount Rushmore National Memorial!"

"I can see it!" Christina squealed. The carved faces of Mount Rushmore hovered over the memorial entrance like four parents watching over their beloved children.

"From so far away they look small!" Grant said.

"Wait till you get closer!" said a familiar voice. Scarlett suddenly appeared through a sea of tourists. "Follow me." Scarlett led the kids through the gateway entrance to the park.

"This place is crowded!" Grant commented.

"More than three million visitors come through the park each year," Scarlett said. "Straight ahead are the Avenue of Flags and then the Grand View Terrace. That's where you will find one of the best views of Mount Rushmore in the whole park!"

They followed Scarlett down an immense entryway lined with soaring columns of stacked gray stone. Flags representing each of the 56 U.S. states and territories dangled from the sides of each column and lapped softly in the wind. Their vivid colors jumped out against the serene gray stone. Christina would normally be fascinated with each state's flag, but she couldn't keep her eyes off the carving that loomed above them.

When they finally arrived at the stone patio of the Grand View Terrace, Christina stood in awe of the view before her. The gray mountain stretched straight toward the sky. Craggy rock and dark green pine trees lined the base of the mountain but ended where the smooth rock began. Four faces in the mountain stared into the bright blue South Dakota sky, each frozen in time.

Christina noticed George Washington first. His face jutted out of the left of the mountain. Coarse mountain rock framed his face, but the carving looked as smooth as polished stone. "George Washington looks kind and concerned, don't you think?" Christina said, to no one in particular. Grant simply nodded, his eyes glued to the mountainside.

Beside Washington, Thomas Jefferson gazed in another direction. He looked just like Christina remembered from her history books. Theodore Roosevelt appeared next, in the back nook of the monument. Even from a distance, Christina could see where the sculptor had outlined the rims of Roosevelt's glasses.

Finally, Christina's eyes rested on Abraham Lincoln on the far right. He had always been her favorite president. "He looks so real," she whispered. "His beard looks like real hair curling into the rock."

"You must be talking about Lincoln," Rory said. "Notice his sunken cheeks and even his mole. That sculptor was amazing."

"I've seen a hundred pictures of Mount Rushmore," Christina said. "But now I know a picture can't do it justice."

"And the faces are so clear, aren't they?" Rory said. "I've been here many times but I can never get over how lifelike the faces are. Sometimes I imagine Old Abe turning his head and talking to us tourists!"

"I think the most amazing thing about Mount Rushmore is the size," Mato said. "Did you know that each face is 60 feet tall? If I could stand on top of myself 12 times, I still wouldn't be as tall as one of those faces!"

"Just the noses look almost as tall as my two-story house in Georgia!" Grant said.

"I told you it wouldn't look small once you got closer," Scarlett said. She'd quietly listened to the kids' conversation. "Since your Mimi needed to get some more research done, she asked me to keep you guys company. Come with me."

Scarlett led the kids down a stairway off to the side of the terrace. On the stairs, Christina realized the Grand View Terrace was actually the roof of another building.

"This is the Lincoln Borglum Museum," Scarlett said. "He was Gutzon's son. Lincoln was the one who finished..." Scarlett hesitated. "We'll just say he carried on his father's work."

Christina and Grant looked at each other, confused. Christina wondered why Scarlett didn't just say that Lincoln finished the carving on Mount Rushmore.

Scarlett led the kids to a door that read "Authorized Park Personnel Only." She whipped out a key, jiggled it in the handle, and pushed the door open.

"Wow!" Grant said. "I feel like I'm going into a top-secret passageway!"

"Don't get too excited," Scarlett said, smiling. "It's just my office." Scarlett led the four down a dimly lit hallway to a small room. Her name appeared on a plaque above the door. The kids shuffled in and plopped down on stiff, cold plastic chairs.

"I want to explain some things," Scarlett said.

Christina began to feel uncomfortable. They were alone with someone they barely knew in a secret building. Suddenly Christina realized she didn't trust Scarlett!

17
SPILL YOUR GUTZ!

Christina fidgeted in her chair as Scarlett spouted off facts about Mount Rushmore. They were all things she read before in history books. Gutzon Borglum started the carving in 1927, and his son, Lincoln, finished it in 1941. The carving cost almost a million dollars. Not one worker died while carving the memorial.

But then, Scarlett said something Christina didn't expect.

"Not everyone knows everything about Mount Rushmore," Scarlett said. Her voice grew quieter. "There are many secrets hidden in this place."

Christina felt the hair rise on the back of her neck.

"Like what?" Grant asked.

"Well, I can't tell you everything," Scarlett continued. "But I can tell you that Mount Rushmore isn't finished, and it probably never will be."

"It isn't finished?" Rory asked, surprised. "I've lived in South Dakota whole my life and I've never heard that."

"Well, it's not always taught in history books," Scarlett continued. "But if you look hard enough, you'll find it. There's even a replica of what the memorial was originally supposed to look like in the Lincoln Borglum Museum."

"What's missing?" Christina asked. She tried to avoid sounding suspicious.

"More than you know," Scarlett replied. Her voice trailed off as if she meant to say it under her breath. "Gutzon Borglum had big plans," Scarlett continued. "He wanted the presidents to be carved all the way to their waists, not just their faces. He also wanted to carve a large inscription into the side of the mountain that explained why he carved Mount Rushmore."

"Why didn't he?" Mato asked.

"The rock was unstable," Scarlett explained. "The inscription would have cracked the rock and put the whole carving in danger."

Grant's eyes widened. He imagined Mount Rushmore crumbling in an avalanche of noses, eyes, hair, and mouths.

"Gutzon wanted to do even more than the inscription," Scarlett continued. "He wanted a place where people could admire the great artifacts of the United States. He wanted..." Scarlett's voice trailed off again.

Christina sensed that Scarlett wasn't telling them everything she knew. Christina wanted to ask questions, but she was afraid to tell Scarlett too much. She couldn't risk

Scarlett knowing about the mystery. Christina squirmed again in her seat. She wished she could escape and get back outside.

Suddenly Scarlett leaned her whole body toward the kids. She eyed each one of them, letting her eyes linger on Christina. Christina held her breath. She could tell Scarlett was about to say something very important.

"Behind the mountain..." Scarlett began, but before she could say any more, sunlight filled the hallway and swept into Scarlett's office.

18
MISSING SIBLING

SQUEEEAAAKKK! Mimi and Papa slowly opened the door to Scarlett's office and squinted to see in the dim light.

"How'd you get in here?" Grant said. He'd never been so excited to see his grandparents.

"Scarlett gave us her spare key so I could use her office for research," Mimi said. "What are you four doing back here?"

Scarlett stood up and dusted off the front of her shirt. "Um, I was just telling the kids some, uh, some important Mount Rushmore facts," she stuttered.

"Isn't that nice!" Mimi said, delighted. "How kind of you to take extra time with these kids!"

"Why don't you kids go outside," Papa boomed. "Mimi and I have some research to discuss with Scarlett."

The kids gladly hurried out of Scarlett's office, down the long hallway, and back into the blazing sunlight.

"Did you hear that?" Christina asked.

"Yeah," Grant said. "Mimi and Papa didn't know Scarlett was taking us back to her office. But Scarlett said Mimi and Papa wanted her to take care of us!"

"She's beginning to creep me out," Rory added.

"No, not that," Christina said. "I'm talking about the last thing Scarlett said before Mimi and Papa so rudely interrupted."

"Rudely interrupted?" Grant said. "Mimi and Papa just saved us from the evil park ranger queen!"

"Christina's right, though," Mato said. "I think Scarlett was about to tell us something really important."

"All she said was 'behind the mountain,'" Rory said. "What does that mean?"

"The clues!" Christina blurted out. "Most of the clues have to do with something behind: 'a face can hide what's really behind'; 'what lurks behind me tells the true story of the country you see'; 'I may be hard as stone, but there's a passage to the center of my heart.' There's got to be something behind Mount Rushmore!"

"But this mountain is huge," Mato said. "Just the base is miles wide. We'd never find whatever the clues are describing!"

"Maybe what we need is one more clue," Grant said. His voice sounded distracted. Grant stepped toward the glass doors of the Lincoln Borglum Museum and pointed to the stone surrounding it. A porcelain tile was plastered near the ground!

"Oh my gosh!" Christina said. "This mystery is getting more and more mysterious."

"That clue isn't even hidden," Mato said. "Anyone could find it down there." Mato watched hundreds of tourists wander around the entrance to the museum.

"But not if they're not looking!" Rory said. "What does it say?"

Grant leaned down and read the black inscription on the tile aloud.

The top's the spot to find me, behind the face lies the treasure that's hiding.

Christina, Mato, and Rory turned and stared at the mountain behind them. It rose hundreds of feet into the air with sharp, steep cliffs. There was no way they could hike to the top.

"I guess that's the end," Christina said. She felt so disappointed. "All these clues and now we can't even find what they're for."

"Sorry, Christina," Mato said. "I love a good adventure, but no one's allowed on the top of Mount Rushmore, especially four kids."

Christina knew the mystery was over. It was the first one she couldn't solve.

"This stinks, doesn't it, Grant?" Christina said.

Her brother was silent.

"Grant?" Christina said again, louder. She still heard no reply.

Christina turned around to look where Grant had stood just moments before. Grant was gone!

19
RACE FOR
MOUNT RUSHMORE

"Grant!" Christina yelled. She began to panic. She strained her eyes over the mass of people, searching for Grant's messy blond hair. There was no sign of him. "Grant's missing!" Christina shouted to Mato and Rory.

"Missing?" Mato said. "He was just here a minute ago."

"I know," Christina huffed. "But now I can't find him!"

"There!" Rory interrupted. She pointed toward a steep nature trail to the side of the tourist area. Christina spotted Grant's bright blond hair and orange T-shirt between the pine tree branches.

"Let's go!" Christina said.

Mato, Rory, and Christina ran to the trail and called after Grant. He didn't stop.

"Grant's too far ahead of us," Mato said. "I don't know if we can catch up."

"Where does he think he's going?" Rory asked.

"To the top," Christina said confidently.

Mato and Rory stopped in their tracks and stared at Christina.

"Why would he do that?" Mato said. "It's crazy!"

"We've never not solved a mystery," Christina said. "I guess Grant doesn't plan on starting now." Even though she was worried about her brother's safety, Christina was proud of his bravery.

"We have to follow him now," Mato said. "We can't let him climb the mountain alone."

The three trudged up the steep path in silence. The trail wrapped around the back of the mountain, then led straight up. Christina's legs burned from the steep incline.

"Someone's been this way before, but not in a long time" Mato commented. The worn trail was barely visible underneath a layer of pine needles.

The pine trees became sparse as the trail got steeper and steeper. Christina had to lean forward and grasp the rock to steady her body. Soon all the trees were below them and a mass of gray rock stretched on ahead.

"GRAAAANT!" Christina yelled. Grant refused to stop or even look back. But he was moving slower and slower as the mountain got steeper.

"I think we can catch up to him now," Mato said. "It looks like he's losing energy."

Mato, Rory, and Christina picked up their pace. Christina's muscles screamed in pain. She wasn't used to mountain climbing!

"Grant!" Christina finally caught up with her brother and yanked his shirt. "What in the world do you think you're doing?"

"T-t-t-trying not to look d-d-down!" Grant stuttered. Christina remembered her brother was terrified of heights.

"What possessed you to climb the mountain?" Mato asked.

"I c-couldn't let this my-mystery go uns-s-solved," Grant said. His voice trembled. "I kn-kn-knew Christina wouldn't let me c-c-come up here!"

"You are right about that!" Christina said.

"So I d-didn't ask!" Grant said. Even though he was scared, Grant managed to give his sister a grin.

"Um, guys," Rory interrupted. "I think our hike just got easier."

Grant and Christina gazed up the steep incline. A crumbly stone staircase stretched all the way to the top of the mountain.

"Someone's *definitely* been here before," Mato said.

Suddenly Scarlett's mysterious secrets seemed very real!

20
HALLWAY OF
HIDDEN HISTORY

Christina counted the stone stairs as she struggled to the top.

"501, 502, 503, 504, 505," Christina recited. She slammed down her foot. "506!" The last step ended at a flat spot in a crevice at the top of the mountain. Christina's whole body shook with exhaustion.

"This way!" Grant said. The stutter in his voice disappeared when he set foot on flat ground.

A path led through the crevice into a wider flat opening.

"I can't believe it," Mato said. He stared at a rounded rock in front of them. Long vertical lines burrowed into the rock. "We're at the top of Mount Rushmore, and *that* is the back of Lincoln's head!"

Christina examined the round rock that jutted in front of them. It was big enough to be its own mountain! "He's HUGE from up here," Christina said. She didn't dare look over the edge to see the rest of the carving.

"What's that?" Rory asked.

Christina and Mato turned to see an opening on the opposite rock wall. It looked like the entrance to a carefully carved square cave. They moved closer. Christina gasped. "Look at that!" she cried.

Just inside the opening, sunlight shimmered off a shiny black stone box with an inscription on top. Behind the box, the opening stretched into a long, dark hallway that ended abruptly in a wall of solid stone.

The walls of the hallway had the same vertical lines that were carved into the back of Lincoln's head.

"Oh my gosh!" Christina said. "We've just found a secret passageway at the back of Mount Rushmore. I can't believe it!"

"I'm not sure it's a secret to everyone," Mato said. He read the inscription on the black box. "It's a quote from Gutzon Borglum."

"Good old Gutzon himself?" Grant asked. "And what are these letters on the side, MCMXCVIII?"

"They're Roman numerals!" Rory said suddenly. "I just learned about them in school. Let's see...that means...nineteen hundred and ninety eight. Nineteen-Ninety-Eight!"

"Like the year?" Grant asked.

"That means this wasn't put here too long ago," Mato said. "I wonder what's inside."

"I don't know, but I'm sure this is what the clues were talking about," Christina said.

"For some reason, someone wanted us to find all this."

Christina stepped into the hallway and ran her fingers along the rough vertical lines. "What are these?" she asked.

"Those are drill marks," Mato said. "The workers who carved Mount Rushmore drilled holes, stuck dynamite in them, and blew off chunks of rock to form the faces. Workers sat on swings hoisted from the top of the mountain so they could get close enough to chisel out details on each president. The same workers who carved the mountain must have made this hallway."

"But it just stops," Rory said. "I wonder why he didn't finish it."

"He didn't get to finish Mount Rushmore, either," Grant said. "Maybe Borglum's 'gutz' were too big for his budget!"

"Huh?" Christina said.

"He means maybe they ran out of money," Mato interpreted.

"Or maybe the rock was unstable, like Scarlett explained," Rory suggested.

The four stared in disbelief at their secret discovery. Christina was amazed, but one thing stuck in her mind. She still couldn't figure out who would want to lead them to the top of Mount Rushmore.

Suddenly the crunch of boots on gravel echoed around the crevice. Someone had followed them to the top!

21
PARK RANGER
DANGER!

Christina stepped in front of Grant to protect him from the coming villain. Just as she braced herself to defend her friends, she saw a red tennis shoe with silver laces sparkle in the sun.

"Grant? Christina?" Mimi said in a panic. She ran to her grandchildren and covered them in a bear hug.

"Mimi?" Christina said. She was beyond confused. Papa came next, followed by Scarlett.

"We couldn't find you anywhere when we finished our research," Mimi said. "Scarlett suggested maybe you'd be here at the top. I didn't know why you would be, but I had to look!"

"I'm sorry...I never...I didn't..." Scarlett repeated over and over. A look of worry creased her already wrinkled face.

"It was you!" Christina pointed at Scarlett. She shrugged away from Mimi. "It was you all along!" Scarlett backed away from Christina's accusing pointed finger.

"You were at Wall Drug Store when we found the first clue," Christina said.

"And Custer State Park!" Mato realized.

"And here!" Grant said.

"They're right. And you were the one who suggested we visit the Badlands and Crazy Horse," Christina continued. "Mimi said you had good suggestions for the best spots to visit. That's how you knew where we'd be every step of the way. You *wanted* us to climb to the top of this mountain. That's why you knew we'd be here when Mimi and Papa couldn't find us."

"But...it was just...." Scarlett stuttered.

"But there's one thing I still can't figure out," Christina said. "Why?"

"Yes, why?" Mimi said. She looked at Scarlett expectantly. "Why would you coax my grandchildren to the top of Mount Rushmore?"

"I *never* meant for this to happen!" Scarlett explained. She looked like she was about to cry. "The clues were something I started long ago in my first year as a park ranger. I decided it might be fun to plant clues at some famous South Dakota landmarks so people could have a scavenger hunt on their vacation. The clues led to the top because I wanted people to learn about something."

Scarlett pointed toward the opening in the rock. "It's called the Hall of Records," she explained. "It's my favorite part of Mount Rushmore, but not many people know it's here."

"What is it?" Grant asked. He was too curious to be suspicious of Scarlett any more.

"It was built by Gutzon Borglum as a continuation of the monument," Scarlett explained. "He wanted to create a long hallway behind the faces that tourists could walk through. He planned to house important U.S. documents like the Constitution and the Declaration of Independence right here at the top of Mount Rushmore. Unfortunately, he never finished it."

"Why?" Rory asked.

"The rock was too dense," Scarlett said. "He was running out of time and money so he decided to focus his efforts on finishing the presidents' faces. He never got to complete his dream."

"But someone knows about it," Mato said. "This black box is dated 1998."

"You're right," Scarlett said. "You kids are smart! The box was dedicated in 1998 to commemorate Gutzon's dream for the Hall of Records. Inside the box are porcelain panels inscribed with important documents like the

Declaration of Independence, the Constitution, and even a history of the four presidents on Mount Rushmore. The inscription was written in tiny writing so the whole document could fit on each panel. One porcelain panel tells Gutzon's story and his reason for creating Mount Rushmore."

"That's why the clues were written on porcelain tiles, isn't it," Christina said.

"That's right," Scarlett admitted. "If someone found all the clues and was smart enough to put them together, it would lead them to the Hall of Records. No one has ever figured it out—not until you kids!"

"But why would you lead someone here if no one is supposed to be here?" Grant asked.

"I planted the clues before I knew the back of the mountain was off limits," Scarlett explained. "I was young and inexperienced. I used to come up here all the time to clean the rock and fill small cracks in with caulk. I figured the stairs where made so tourists could see the top of the mountain. I later found out the stairs were used by the workers in the 1920s and 1930s and no one was allowed up here but park staff. I should have gotten rid of the clues long ago, but I just thought no one would figure it out. Honest!"

Christina felt a twinge of guilt for accusing Scarlett so harshly. She believed Scarlett never meant to cause any harm.

"Well, we better get down off this rock," Papa suggested. "It'll be dark soon enough."

The group headed back to the stairs for the long hike down. As Christina walked away, she glanced one last time at the Hall of Records. She was glad she could see Gutzon Borglum's dream come true, even if it wasn't quite finished.

22
BIG HEAD!

"Whew! I'm beat," Grant said. "Nothing like climbing an entire mountain to work up an appetite!"

Grant and Christina were glad to be back on level ground at the Grand View Terrace. They'd made it down the mountain just as the sky turned dark. The giant faces in the distance were barely visible in the night sky.

Scarlett felt horrible about putting the kids in danger, but Mimi and Papa assured her she was forgiven on one condition—she had to get rid of all her clues! In gratitude, Scarlett suggested the four stay for her specialty, the Mount Rushmore Evening Lighting Ceremony. She made one last apology and hurried off to help run the lighting show.

"She really was a nice lady," Christina said. "I thought that from the beginning, but then I just got too caught up in the mystery."

Suddenly, a spotlight revealed Theodore Roosevelt's face on the mountain. The stone cast a soft white glow in the dark night. One by one, spotlights clicked on each president from Thomas Jefferson to Abraham Lincoln to George Washington. More and more spotlights blazed brighter and brighter until the whole mountain glowed in a shower of light.

"It really is beautiful," Christina said. She leaned against Mimi's shoulder and sighed. "I'm going to miss this place and my new friends."

Mato and Rory had to say goodbye when they reached the bottom of the mountain. Mato said his dad expected them home by dark. Mato, Rory, Grant, and Christina promised to keep in touch, but Christina still felt sad.

"I know, sweetie," Mimi said. "I love these wide, open spaces!"

Christina breathed in a long breath of fresh prairie air. "It's just not the same back home," she said.

"Well, I'm ready for home," Grant said. "I've got a stuffed jackalope to show off to all my friends! I'll have them fooled in no time!"

Mimi laughed. "One thing's for sure, you two know how to scare your poor grandmother," she said.

"I think climbing up a mountain was enough scare for the whole year," Papa said. He smiled at Grant and patted him on the back. "But I have to say, son, you sure were brave!"

"After today, I think you conquered your fear of heights!" Mimi told Grant.

"I don't know about th-th-that," Grant said. He started to stutter just thinking about the mountain.

"Grant played a big part in figuring out our mystery," Christina said. "Without him we would never have climbed the mountain, found the Hall of Records, or realized Scarlett planted the clues."

"What can I say?" Grant said, crossing his arms confidently. "I'm a bit of a pro at this whole mystery thing."

"Now, Grant, don't go and get a big head," Christina said.

"I think I might like a big head," Grant said thoughtfully. "Then I could end up on the mountain with those other big-headed guys!"

Christina, Mimi, and Papa gazed at the glowing presidential faces in the distance. They began to giggle, picturing Grant's curly blonde head etched in stone.

"You'd definitely need a 'makeover' before I'd let that happen," Mimi said, "including a haircut, teeth cleaning, and a good old face scrubbing!"

"Aww, never mind then," Grant decided. "I think I like being a little boy with a little head just fine!"

Now...go to
www.carolemarshmysteries.com
and...

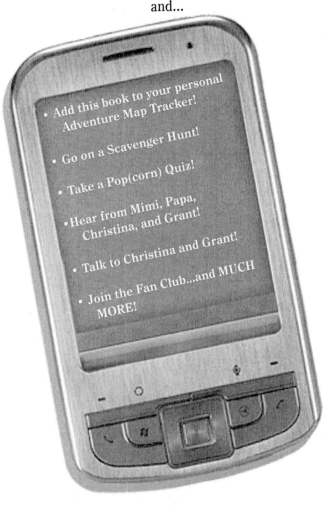

- Add this book to your personal Adventure Map Tracker!

- Go on a Scavenger Hunt!

- Take a Pop(corn) Quiz!

- Hear from Mimi, Papa, Christina, and Grant!

- Talk to Christina and Grant!

- Join the Fan Club...and MUCH MORE!

GLOSSARY

dynamite: explosive

mesmerized: to keep your full attention on something, to be fascinated

Panama Canal: a man-made canal that allows boats to pass from the Atlantic Ocean to the Pacific Ocean

paralyzed: not able to move

prairie: a flat, grassy plain with dry soil and few trees

savor: enjoy; receive pleasure from

sculptor: an artist who creates three-dimensional artwork from a variety of materials, including rock, marble, metal, glass, and wood

SAT GLOSSARY

acreage: area of land measured in acres (an acre is about the size of a football field minus the end zones)

demonstrate: to show clearly

subterfuge: a deception or something used to conceal or escape

suspicious: to doubt or mistrust the honesty of something or someone

uproot: to remove by the roots

Enjoy this exciting excerpt from:

THE MYSTERY ON THE

Oregon Trail

1
GATEWAY TO THE WEST

Grant squished his face against the rectangular glass window and squinted. He shoved his messy blond hair away from his eyes.

"I think I can see Independence from here!" he said. He whirled around to have Mimi look and bumped right into Christina.

"OUCH!" Christina cried. "Um, that was my foot."

"Sorry, but I think I can see Independence from here," Grant insisted. "Look!"

Christina glared out the window, squinting her eyes against the sunlight.

"Nope, I don't think so. Independence is too far away," she said.

"But I know that's..." Grant argued.

"We'll be there soon enough," Mimi interrupted. "You two just enjoy the view. It's spectacular! They say you can see for 30 miles on a clear day like today!"

Grant and Christina couldn't argue with their grandmother because the view was amazing. They were standing 630 feet in the air at the top of the Gateway Arch in St. Louis, Missouri—the official start of the Oregon Trail. Grant felt like he was on top of the world!

"Did you know," Mimi began, "that the Gateway Arch is twice as tall as the Statue of

Liberty and the tallest national monument in the United States?"

Grant shook his head silently, still mesmerized by the view. Christina watched the people below moving around like tiny floating toys. Her eyes scanned the flat western land she'd soon be traveling—not by car or bus or train—but by covered wagon!

"The view may be spectacular," said Papa in his booming voice, "but it sure is high up here."

"Come on, Papa," said Christina, "you're the cowboy pilot! You fly the *Mystery Girl* all over the world. You can't be afraid of heights!"

"Well, I'm in control of the *Mystery Girl* when I fly," Papa explained. "This arch is entirely different!"

Grant and Christina giggled at Papa's anxious expression. It was funny, and rare, to see him nervous in his big cowboy hat and tough leather boots. Grant and Christina knew their grandparents well and often traveled with them. Mimi was a children's mystery book writer, and Papa flew her anywhere she needed to go in his red-and-white plane, the *Mystery Girl*.

Suddenly, the tour guide chimed in on the intercom. "Thank you for visiting the Gateway Arch, America's Gateway to the West!"

That was their cue to make room for the next group of eager tourists. Grant and Christina gladly made their way to the tram that would take them on the steep return ride to the ground.

"Here we go again—the worst part of the whole trip," Papa grumbled. The ride to the top of the arch had not gone so well for Papa and Mimi. The family was crammed together in a little egg-shaped pod that zoomed up the inside of the arch. Mimi felt a bit faint and Papa's face was a bright shade of fire-truck red the entire time.

"What do you mean, Papa?" Grant asked. "The ride up to the top was the best part!" He grinned at Christina, who was also looking forward to the rollercoaster ride back down the arch.

"Yeah," Christina said, "maybe we'll get stuck!"

"Stuck?" Mimi asked, alarmed.

"Before we got here," Christina explained, "I read online that just a couple of years ago, the power went out in the tram. People were stuck in the thing for hours!"

"And that makes you excited?" Mimi asked, creasing her eyebrows in a frown.

"Oh, Mimi, it would be an adventure!" said Grant with a mischievous smile. "You love adventures!"

"Not that kind of adventure!" Mimi replied, almost shouting.

"No, sir-eee," Papa drawled. "An adventure like that is more of a BADventure!"

Grant and Christina giggled as their uneasy grandparents stepped into their tram car. Before the doors shut, Grant took one last look out the rectangular windows lining the inside of the arch.

"The Wild West! I can't wait!" he exclaimed. "Yee Haw!"

2
HOME ON THE RANGE

Christina slowly opened her eyes. Her long, shiny, brown hair stuck to her face with sweat. The sun blared down in the backseat of Mimi and Papa's rental car. Their drive from St. Louis to Independence, Missouri took longer than she expected and she must have dozed off. The last time she looked out the window, the scenery consisted of skyscrapers, rivers, and highways. Now, she saw nothing but flat land, grass, and dust—lots of dust!

Christina glanced at the seat next to her where Grant was busy clicking away on his video game. Christina nudged his side with her elbow.

"Hey, Grant, have you seen where we are?" she asked.

"Yeah, it's the prairie, duh!" Grant said, never taking his bright blue eyes off the video game screen. "You've been asleep forever!"

"It's a good thing you got some sleep, Christina," Papa said from the front seat. "We've got a lot of work ahead of us."

"Speaking of work," said Mimi, "there's the sign for Independence city limits right there!"

Christina watched the sign whoosh by and fade away as they sped down the highway.

"What is *that*?" Grant asked, pointing off to the side of the road at a long line of giant, white arches covering boxy, wooden wagons. In the front of each wagon were two horses attached with harnesses. They kicked at the dusty ground with their rough hooves and whinnied across the quiet prairie.

"That's a train of prairie schooners," said Mimi.

"Prairie whats?" Grant asked, confused.

"Schooners," Mimi replied. "*Prairie Schooner* was the nickname given to covered wagons..."

"I know why, Mimi!" Christina said, interrupting Mimi in the middle of her sentence.

"All right, why?" Mimi asked, adjusting the sparkly red sunglasses perched on her nose.

"Because the white wagon tops look like sails from boats floating across the prairie," Christina explained.

"You're absolutely correct," Mimi said with a big smile. "Someone's done their research on the Oregon Trail!"

Christina glanced at Grant with raised eyebrows. He frowned.

"Well, I don't need to do research," Grant said, "I know how to be a real cowboy just like Papa. It comes natural!"

Papa nodded at Grant in the rear view mirror and grinned as he pulled the car to a stop. Grant and Christina jumped out of the car and raced toward the wagons.

"Whoa! Look at those wheels!" said Grant.

"Yeah, they're huge!" said Christina. "And these must be our clothes for the trip." Her expression changed as she held up two plain, scratchy, cotton dresses and two pairs of chocolate-brown work trousers with white shirts.

"Great, real stylish," Christina groaned and carried the larger dress to Mimi. She tried to imagine Mimi in a bland, cotton dress, much different from the trendy clothes and sparkly glasses she usually wore. Christina wondered if Mimi was cut out for life on the open range.

Mimi winked at her granddaughter. "This will be a new look for us," she said. "Isn't 'retro' the new fashion trend these days?"

Grant skipped back to the car to help Papa unload their supplies for the wagon. Papa pulled out blankets, a shovel, a barrel for water, a chest of extra clothes and shoes, and some pots, pans, and plates.

"Where's the TV?" said Grant.

Papa peered at Grant from beneath the brim of his jet-black cowboy hat.

"There's no electricity on the trail, Grant," he explained. "How would you watch TV?"